George Webb Medley, Cobden Club

The Reciprocity Craze

A tract for the times

George Webb Medley, Cobden Club

The Reciprocity Craze
A tract for the times

ISBN/EAN: 9783337406141

Printed in Europe, USA, Canada, Australia, Japan

Cover: Foto ©Andreas Hilbeck / pixelio.de

More available books at **www.hansebooks.com**

PRICE THREEPENCE.

THE

RECIPROCITY CRAZE.

A Tract for the Times.

BY

GEORGE W. MEDLEY.

CASSELL, PETTER, GALPIN & CO.:

LONDON, PARIS & NEW YORK.

1881.

THE

RECIPROCITY CRAZE.

A Tract for the Times.

BY

GEORGE W. MEDLEY.

CASSELL, PETTER, GALPIN & CO.:

LONDON, PARIS & NEW YORK.

1881.

CONTENTS.

PAGE

I. INTRODUCTION 5

II. IMPORTS AND EXPORTS (" *Pons asinorum* ') . 6

III. ONE-SIDED FREE TRADE 14

IV. " RECIPROCITY OR RETALIATION " 24

V. TWO NEO-PROTECTIONISTS 26
    1. A Quarterly Reviewer.
    2. Sir Edward Sullivan, Bart., *Nineteenth Century*

VI. CONCLUSION 35

THE RECIPROCITY CRAZE.

I.

INTRODUCTION.

FOR some time past incessant attacks have been made on our Free Trade policy. At first these attacks were made doubtingly, hesitatingly ; but lately, speakers and writers have become emboldened, the banner of "Protection to Native Industry" has once more been unfurled, and the air resounds with cries for "Reciprocity or Retaliation." This is an astonishing phenomenon to those who understand and appreciate what Free Trade has done, and is doing, for this country. The most striking feature about the agitation is, to their minds, its extraordinary inopportuneness ; the time chosen for it being just that moment when the clouds of depression are dispersing, and we seem to be once more floating on the rising wave of prosperity. We have now had thirty-five years' experience of Free Trade, with their ups and downs of inflation and depression. In the course of these years we have witnessed all sorts of political and social changes. We have seen the overthrow of dynasties, the uprising of peoples, and wars waged on an unprecedented scale. Railways and telegraphs have obviated to a great extent the inconveniences of distance and time. Great perturbations in the standard of value have occurred, the gold discoveries at first causing a general rise in prices. Of late years, however, an increasing demand for the metal, and a diminishing supply, accompanied by a partial demonetisation of silver, have caused a disturbance of values in the opposite direction of a general fall in prices. During all these years, England alone among the nations has maintained a system of free ports, the only changes in her fiscal policy being in the direction of greater freedom, while other nations, such as the United States, France, and Germany, have raised round themselves the barriers of prohibitory tariffs. With one exception, every conceivable economical condition that could constitute a test of the principles and practice of Free Trade has occurred, the one condition untried being universal Free Trade. In these circumstances, and with all this varied experience, one would suppose that there was not much room for differences of opinion as to the results achieved, and as to our national condition at the end of the ordeal. Yet, from what is passing around, we cannot but see that extreme divergences exist. While, on the one hand, the Free Trader contemplates with satisfaction the position which his country has attained by her commercial policy, and appeals with confidence to the facts which abound on every side, and which, to his mind, verify to the fullest the theories he has embraced ; on the other we find a school of neo-protectionists lamenting what seems to them to be the decadence of their country, and appealing also to facts which appear to them to bear out their views. But, the most astounding thing is, that some of the very same facts which are appealed to by one party as evidence of our abounding prosperity, are held up by the other as the certain proofs of our decay ! A crucial example of this is to be found in the various conclusions drawn from the figures which appear in our Board of Trade Returns under the head of " Imports and Exports." The views of the writer upon this and other cognate subjects are, of course, those of the Free Trader. They are set forth in the following chapters in a manner which, it is hoped, will be sufficiently clear. They may perhaps aid the candid inquirer in a search for the truth, and tend to dissipate the " craze."

II.

IMPORTS AND EXPORTS.

" Pons Asinorum."

THE fact that year after year the money value of our imports vastly exceeds the money value of our exports, and that this excess tends to increase is, to many minds, not only a puzzle, but a rock of offence, and a cause of alarm. To those, however, who are acquainted with the facts and circumstances which cause this excess, nothing can seem more absurd than the feeling which has been aroused, and the conclusions which have been drawn. The absurdity will be made abundantly clear as we proceed.

But, I must here warn the reader that he will have to master what I have to say under this head, for it constitutes the "Pons Asinorum" of the Free Trade question. If he passes this "pons," he will find himself among the Free Traders on the other side. If not, he must be numbered among the Neo-Protectionists, who seem to be utterly unable to pass over it. This is what they cannot get over :—They point to the Board of Trade returns for 1880, which show that we imported £411,000,000 worth of commodities, and exported only £286,000,000 worth ; and this they call a balance of trade against us of £125,000,000 ; and from this fact they draw such deductions as these : that this balance is a loss to the country ; that John Bull *buys* £411,000,000 of goods from the foreigner, and *sells* him only £286,000,000 worth ; that, consequently, the foreigner has the best of the trade ; that he is draining away all John Bull's wealth ; that the latter is getting poorer and poorer ; that if the system goes on it must end in his ruin ; and that this is the outcome of the one-sided Free Trade now existing. And then they give vent in their agony to such cries as " Protection to Native Industry," "Reciprocity or Retaliation." Here are some of their utterances :—

The Quarterly Review, July 1881, p. 293.—"In 1846 our imports amounted to little more than 74 millions ; in 1850, when Sir Robert Peel died, they reached 100½ millions. Last year they were valued at 410 millions. Did Sir Robert Peel ever dream of such an import trade as this? If he did, it is most probable he saw in his dreams our exports approaching the same standard if not exceeding it, and that such a balance sheet as the following never rose up before his mind's eye :—

" Imports in 1880	...	...	...	£409,990,056
" Exports ,, ,,	...	...	...	222,810,526

" Excess of Imports 187,179,530

This excess, according to the writers we have quoted, represents the sum by which we have grown more wealthy in 1880 than we were in 1879. Is it possible that any one with a mind capable of comprehending facts and their meaning can really believe it?"

Ib. p. 288.—To buy more than we sell, and to make that not a mere accident of our trade but its permanent condition—the end above all others to be sought for and desired—this, according to the economists is a most excellent thing for the country. Practical men who look at such matters from a strictly-business point of view, come to a different conclusion. They hold that we cannot persevere in this system without plunging the country into disaster. . . . As one authority (Mr. Shaw-Lefevre, M.P., 27th June, 1878) puts it, 'the magnitude of our import trade, so far from being a matter for alarm, is evidence of the greatness of our resources and the stability of our position.' This is one of the most blundering and most mischievous of the delusions which have helped to blind a portion of the people to the true state of their affairs."

Sir Edward Sullivan, Bart., *Nineteenth Century*, August, 1881. p. 171.—" It [Isolated Free Trade] has enabled foreigners to flood our markets with cheap, and often nasty manufactured goods." " It has increased the balance of trade against us, till it has reached the alarming figure of £136,000,000." P. 176.—" In the face of these facts we are warranted in again asking our economic philosophers how we are to continue to find money to purchase foreign food. The food question is at the bottom of our commercial troubles ; we are buying food from abroad faster than we are making money to pay for it. But of course this cannot last. Until the immense and increasing excess of imports over exports, is considerably diminished, there can be no return of general prosperity. We may for a time draw upon our capital and our accumulated wealth, but for how long ? If we cannot get as much for our goods as we are compelled to pay for foreign food, the deluge must be at hand."

Nothing can be more clear and distinct than the issues

which these statements **raise.** I shall at once address **myself to** them, merely remarking, in passing, that under **the head of** "Two Neo-Protectionists," I shall have to make further reference to the articles from which I have quoted.

The first thing that strikes one regarding these utterances is this—that **the** bare fact of our imports being larger than **our** exports is **held** by these writers to constitute in itself a great and growing evil. According to them it is a self-evident proposition, the mere propounding of which ought to carry conviction **to** every mind. And on this **idea** their whole argument seems to be **based.** They **leave** out of account everything but the **bare** fact that **our imports** exceed our exports! They leave out of account **such** matters as the following:—Our shipping receipts, in-surance, interest, merchants' profits, and, last not least, **the income we** derive from our foreign investments! Let us try **to** make **a** rough estimate of these "unconsidered trifles."

As regards shipping, we possessed **in** 1880 56 per cent. of **the** world's ocean carrying power; assuming that the average of freight is about 10 per cent. *ad valorem*, and our combined export and import trade is about 700 millions, our receipts under this head may **be put** down at **40** millions; but to this must be added the receipts for our inter-foreign and inter-colonial trade, and the receipts from passenger traffic. I do not think 45 millions a high figure **to** set down as our total shipping receipts. Mulhall, in his "Balance Sheet of the World," p. 44, puts them down at £51,920,000.

Then comes insurance. An average of ½ per cent. on **our** total trade gives £3,500,000.

Next comes interest. If we take the moderate sum of 100 millions **as** employed in our foreign trade, **5 per** cent. gives us 5 millions.

Next come merchants' profits. Say 2½ per cent. on the 700 millions: **this gives us** 17½ millions.

Lastly, **take** foreign investments. The *Economist*, of March 5th last, quoting from the "Bankers' Magazine," puts these down as yielding over 55 millions per annum.

What is **the** total of these items?

Ocean carrying trade	...	...	...	£45,000,000
Insurance	..	...	...	3,500,000
Interest on capital	...	...	...	5,000,000
Merchants' profits	...	...	...	17,500,000
Income from foreign investments		...	...	55,000,000
				£126,000,000

Which means simply this—that before England has to exchange a pound's worth of her own products for a pound's worth of foreign products, she has to receive annually, in some shape or other, over 100 million pounds from the foreigner!

And thus bursts the bubble of our adverse balance of trade! The balance, if there be such a thing, seems to be the other way! And it must be the other way.

It is a matter of common knowledge, or ought to be, that year by year, on the whole, the world grows more and more indebted to us. Year by year we have more and more of the world's obligations in our strong box.

The fallacy under which our Neo-Protectionists labour lies in the terms " buying of the foreigner," " selling to the foreigner."

They fancy that our imports are what we " buy " and our exports what we " sell ; " and, that as there is an excess of the former there is a balance of trade against us, which, somehow or other, out of our wealth, we have to liquidate, and that this process impoverishes the country.

But, as I have shown, there is no balance to liquidate, so there can be no impoverishment ; and so their argument is exploded.

But, let us for a moment look at their supposition in another light. Why should the bare fact of our importing 411 millions of commodities in exchange for 286 millions be held, *ipso facto*, to involve a loss?

To get in more than one gives out seems, *primâ facie*, to ordinary minds, the only way of making a profit! It cannot be pretended that Great Britain stood indebted at the end of 1880 for the excess of imports. There can be no doubt that at that period the world was as much, if not more, indebted to her than at the end of 1879.

But 1880 does not stand alone in its excess of imports. The same thing has gone on for the last thirty-five years.

In 1856 the excess was 43 millions; in 1880 this figure, with interruptions, had risen to 125 millions. Let me ask, out of what fund have we liquidated all these supposed adverse balances?

Then let me ask, what would our Neo-Protectionists say if the products of our industry were annually exported to the extent of 411 millions, and we received back from the foreigner only 286 millions worth in exchange?

Look at the question in yet another light. How can it be otherwise than that our imports should exceed in value our exports? If a merchant export £100 worth of goods, and in exchange for them imports goods worth only £100, he must make a dead loss under the heads of freight, insurance, interest, and profits.

How can it be otherwise?

Let us suppose the goods cost him £100 at Liverpool. He exports them to some foreign country, and, of course, has to pay freight and insurance. Let us say this comes to 10 per cent. On arrival at the foreign market the goods must therefore be worth £110. They must be sold, of course, and let us suppose the proceeds re-invested in goods for importation here. Again comes in the charge for freight, another 10 per cent., which, added to the £110, makes the goods worth £121 on arrival at our ports, independently of interest on the money used, and what the merchant may lay on as profit.

And so the £100 of exports comes back as £121 at least, of imports, and must do so as long as trade is carried on.

And, on this showing, what becomes of complaints founded on the bare fact of our imports exceeding our exports, such as—

That the balance of trade is against us!

That we are being ruined!

That Free Trade is a complete failure!

And now, with reference to this last assertion, let us for a few moments contemplate some of the facts and figures which the records of the last quarter of a century afford us.

I will first take the figures of the years 1870 to 1880, as comprising the latest periods of inflation and depression

then I will take in the whole period from 1854 to 1880,
1854 being the earliest year for which I possess the statistics.
Now, what have we done between 1870 and 1880?

The Board of Trade returns record our

Imports for these eleven years as	...	£4,016,842 814
And our exports as	..	3,022,305,973
Leaving an excess of imports	...	£994,536,841

Did we pay away any gold for this excess? **Let us see.**
The returns show that in these years

We imported of gold and silver ..	..	£341,487,134
And exported	..	305,820,304
Leaving a balance in our hands of	..	£35,666,830

A result achieved during an unprecedented demand for
gold throughout the world, owing to the currency require-
ments of the United States, Germany, Holland, and other
states.

This ought to stagger our Neo-Protectionists; but if not,
I have yet another factor to bring into our calculation, and
that is our foreign loan and investment account.

Having no official records to refer to, I can only make
a rough estimate as to the probable balance of our trans-
actions in this respect during the period in question.

In this time probably 500 millions of foreign loans were
floated in London; and supposing that we took one-half of
these, besides purchasing enormous amounts of United
States securities, and investing in all sorts of industrial
enterprises abroad, I do not think we should be very far
from the mark if we put down the figure at which we have
made the world our debtor during these eleven years as
350 millions. How will John Bull's external balance-sheet
for these years then stand?

He has imported and appropriated of the world's products, *on balance* ...	...	£994,536,841
He has pocketed in bullion, *on balance*	...	35,666,830
He has lent creation, *on balance* ...	...	350,000,000
		1,380,203,671

And in the face of these facts we are asked to believe that we are plunging yearly into disaster !

The figures of the last twenty-seven years are still more startling.

In 1854 our imports amounted to	£152,389,053
In 1880, with interruptions, they had mounted to	411,229,565
In 1854 our exports amounted to	115,821,092
In 1880, with interruptions, they had mounted to	286,414,466

The totals for these twenty-seven years are :—

Imports	... ...	£7,626,503,082
Exports	... ...	5,883,766,072
Excess of imports	... ...	1,742,737,010

The bullion records before me show that from 1860 to 1880 inclusive, we imported, on balance, £83,000,000, or at the rate of about four millions a year. I have no figures for previous years, but we may reckon, from common knowledge, that as from 1854 to 1859 gold flowed into this country in greater quantities, and remained here in larger quantities than since, probably eight millions a year remained here on balance ; so that for the whole twenty-seven years we probably retained £131,000,000 of it.

We will now look at the foreign loan and investment account for this period.

As before stated, we receive by way of interest an annual sum of fifty-five millions.

This capitalised at $4\frac{1}{2}$ per cent. makes over 1,200 millions. And assuming that during the period in question we acquired only one-half of these bonds, &c., the account will stand thus for John Bull :—

He has imported and appropriated of the world's products, *on balance* ...	£1,742,737,010
He has pocketed in bullion, *on balance* ...	131,000,000
He has made Creation his debtor *on balance*	600,000,000
	2,473,737,010

In the course of these twenty-seven years, therefore, we seem to have got hold of the world's products to the amount stated for less than nothing ; for, besides getting these products, we have actually acquired a vast sum in money, and have also induced every civilised nation on earth to give us I O U's., amounting in the aggregate to at least 600 millions sterling ! And, with these facts in our possession, we cannot but see that all the talk we hear about "buying more than we sell" and "our adverse balance of trade" is nothing but arrant nonsense ; and that it is not the Free Traders, but the Neo-Protectionists, who cherish "blundering and mischievous delusions."

III.

ONE-SIDED FREE TRADE.

HAVING safely passed our "pons" we will now, by the help of what this has taught us, examine what our Neo-Protectionists call One-sided Free Trade.

I hold it to mean that while every nation has a free sale for its products in our home markets, we are excluded more or less from some of the great markets of the world by hostile and prohibitory tariffs. This is the truth, but the inferences and conclusions drawn therefrom by our Neo-Protectionists are as false and absurd as their notions about our adverse balance of trade.

They suppose that Great Britain is the principal if not the only sufferer from this state of things ; and they assert that while Protection is advancing the prosperity of other countries, Free Trade is destroying ours.

Free Traders deny these propositions, and, on the contrary, affirm that Free Trade has been, and is, a source of vast prosperity, and an unmitigated blessing to the country, and that Protection has been, and is, a source of loss to those countries which have established it.

Let us now see what we, as a nation, have done under our one-sided Free Trade.

First, let us try and understand the meaning of the complaint that every nation has a free sale for its products in our home markets. From the terms used, it must be evident that every nation which produces anything, and wishes to sell it to us, has to compete with every other nation wishing to do the same thing. It is therefore impossible for us to get the commodities we want cheaper than we do through this universal competition.

No other nation enjoys the advantages which flow from this state of things. We find constantly that commodities are cheaper here than in the countries which produce them. The poor among us are thus enabled to fight the battle of life on the most favourable terms possible. Our labourers are thus fed, housed, and clothed, as cheaply as possible. They are thus enabled to produce cheaply, more cheaply than any other workers ; so cheaply that they have become the dread of every Protectionist nation :—so cheaply that *ad valorem* duties of 50 to 200 per cent. on their productions are inadequate to keep them out of Protectionist markets ; so cheaply, that we almost monopolise, as a matter of cheapness, every neutral market ; so cheaply that we have managed to obtain nearly five-eighths of the world's ocean carrying trade, and are daily driving out of employment such of the remaining vessels as belong to Protectionist nations.

Our one-sided Free Trade has done all this for us, at all events. And no Protectionist nation can divest us of what we have thus got. And of the advantages we enjoy we cannot be deprived except in one way—by other nations becoming also Free Traders.

It must be clear, that so far as our one side goes, it is a very good side, and cannot be improved. Ought we not to be extremely careful how we touch it ? I am going to ask presently why we should touch it ? The Neo-Protectionist would probably say, "because we want to get the other side also."

Are we quite sure this other side will be as good as that we have ? I doubt it.

The complaint is that by hostile tariffs, our productions are excluded from the principal markets of the world. This is true, and on cosmopolitan grounds, and in the interests of humanity, this state of things is to be regretted. But we are not now considering the interests of humanity, we are trying to see how we can advance the particular interests of Great Britain.

There are good reasons for supposing that the existing state of things is not to be regretted by us from the selfish national point of view.

I am not sure, as some are, that Great Britain would in the long run be a gainer by universal Free Trade, and I now start this as a question worthy of calm discussion.

If universal Free Trade existed, its vital and energetic principle, division of labour, would, of course, have full play, and mankind would by its means achieve the maximum of production at the minimum of cost.

I am not quite certain that, as a nation, we should, under it, be absolutely, or comparatively, as well off as we are now.

Let us for a moment imagine all hostile tariffs suddenly abolished.

Has any one ever seriously considered the possible effects, immediate, and remote, which might arise?

Among them would be :—

1. A sudden and vast demand for labour at home.

2. A sudden and a great increase in wages.

3. A rapid increase in the number of our factories, workshops, mills, furnaces, &c.

4. A rampant speculation in everything connected with trade and manufactures.

5. A general rise in prices distressful to those with fixed incomes.

6. A rush of population from home and abroad to our manufacturing centres.

7. A stimulus given to marriage and population.

8. A demoralisation of our labouring classes.

9. Strikes for an increase of wages.

10. The culmination of the foregoing.

11. The beginning of a reaction owing to the commencement of foreign competition.

12. The commencement of a fall in prices.

13. Labour disputes, and strikes against the fall.

14. Progress of the fall in prices.

15. Failures of millowners and manufacturers; closing of mills and factories, and blowing out of furnaces.

16. Labourers thrown out of employment, and consequent increase of pauperism and crime.

17. Extreme depression takes place.

18. The usual healing courses have to be **followed**.

19. After some years of suffering things **settle** down pretty much as they were.

All this is based on the sudden opening of foreign ports. A gradual opening would, of course, modify the process, but the ultimate result would not be different. One of the results which would most probably happen is, **that our** population might be increased by two or three **millions** more than it otherwise would be. But then several questions arise, such as :—" Would the nation then be absolutely or comparatively better off?"

Free Trade introduced into Protectionist countries **would** disorganise their industries—ruin some of them—and **cause** a general displacement of capital **and** labour. Effects the converse of those described as happening **with us** would take place with them. At last a basis would **be found.** Then would arise everywhere a **real** and keen competition with us. Is it quite certain **we** should **come** out **of** it victorious? Take such industries **as** these : **Our** cotton and wool manufactures, our iron manufactures, **our** ocean-carrying trade.

The United States grow cotton, and in Alabama this cotton is adjacent to the iron and **coal** which are produced there and in the neighbouring states. Would our cotton lords and ironmasters view with equanimity the contest with our cousins which would commence on the morrow of the opening of their ports? It might turn out that these cousins might find out some way of making cotton goods and iron as cheap as, or cheaper than, we can. If the competition of foreigners be keen now, notwithstanding **the** weight they carry in the shape of enhanced cost of production, arising out of Protectionist tariffs, what would it be should the weight be removed? What would become of our ship-building and ocean-carrying trade? What would become of **our** trade with the States? What would become of us in neutral markets? **What** would **become of us in** our own markets?

At present, as regards cheapness of production, we stand supreme everywhere in all these things. Protection, in this

respect, handicaps and kills our competitors. Free Trade
would breathe life into them. I say, therefore, speaking
selfishly as an Englishman, we had better remain as we are,
and " let sleeping dogs lie."

But I want to know what it is our Neo-Protectionists
have to lay at the door of Free Trade, even one-sided
Free Trade.

Let us do a little more national stock-taking, for there is
no other way of seeing how we get on.

Under the head " Imports and Exports," I gave figures
which show the grand external results of our one-sided free
trade. Let us now look at our internal condition, and see
whether we can recognise any moral and material progress.

Let us take—1. Population. 2. Pauperism. 3. Crime.
4. Education. 5. Thrift. 6. Bankruptcy. 7. Taxation. 8.
National Debt. 9. Banking. 10. Railways. 11. Agriculture.

1.—POPULATION.

In 1850 the United Kingdom numbered 27,523,694
,, 1860   ,,   ,,   ,,   28,778,411
,, 1870   ,,   ,,   ,,   31,205,444
,, 1880   ,,   ,,   ,,   34,468,552
,, 1881   ,,   ,,   ,,   34,788,814

There is nothing discouraging here, surely. During the
last ten years 3,275,000 persons, nearly 900 a day, have
been added to our population, notwithstanding emigration,
and a protracted agricultural and trade depression.

What is the economical condition of this population?
The following tables will indicate this :—

Years.	Exports.	Per head of Population.			Imports.	Per head of Population.			Excess of Imports per head.		
		£	s.	d.		£	s.	d.	£	s.	d.
1854	115,821,092	4	3	7	152,389,053	5	10	2	1	6	7
1860	164,521,351	5	14	4	210,530,873	7	7	0	1	12	8
1870	244,080,577	7	16	5	303,257,493	9	14	4	1	17	11
1880	286,414,466	8	6	1	411,229,565	11	18	7	3	12	6

Bearing in mind what was said under "Imports and Exports," a glance at this table shows that, fast as our population has increased, its command of wealth, and purchasing power in the world's markets has increased still faster ; and that they exercised this power may be seen by the following table, which shows the consumption per head of population of some of those articles which our working classes consume most :—

CONSUMPTION PER HEAD OF POPULATION OF IMPORTED AND EXCISEABLE ARTICLES.

			1870.	1875.	1880.
Imported only, and exclusive of native.	Bacon	lbs.	1·98	8·26	15·96
	Butter	,,	4·15	4·92	7·42
	Cheese	,,	3·67	5·46	5·66
	Potatoes	,,	2·80	16·05	31·63
	Wheat	,,	122·90	197·08	210·42
Rice		,,	6·74	11·68	14·14
Sugar (raw)		,,	41·40	53·97	54·22
Sugar (refined)		,,	5·83	8·88	9·46
Tea		,,	3·81	4·44	4·59
Spirits imported and excisable		gals.	1·01	1·30	1·09
Malt (British) bushels			1·84	1·95	1·65(1879)

Now let us take pauperism.

2.—PAUPERISM.

Ireland.

1870	Number of Paupers First weeks in January	73,921
1873	,, ,,	79,649
1878	,, ,,	85,530
1879	,, ,,	91,807
1880	,, ,,	100,856
1881	,, ,,	109,655

Scotland.

1870	14th May	126,187
1873	,,	111,996
1878	,,	94,671
1879	,,	97,676
1880	,,	98,608

England and Wales.

Year.	Population.	No. of Paupers January 1.
1850 ...	17,773,324 ...	920,543
1860 ...	19,902,713 ...	851,020
1870 ...	22,457,366 ...	1,079,391
1877 ...	24,547,309	728,350
1878 ...	24,854,397 ...	742,703
1879 ...	25,165,336 ...	800,426
1880 ...	25,480,161 ...	837,940
1881 ...	25,798,922 ...	803,126

These tables also tell their own tale, we see :—

1. That while agriculture remains depressed, trade is reviving, the figures for 1880 and 1881 for England and Wales bringing the fact into strong relief; 2, that as while in 1870 this part of the kingdom had a million of paupers to support, in 1881 it has only 800,000, although the population has in the meantime increased 3,340,000, a marvellous proof of progress; 3, that we appear to be once more embarked on the rising wave of prosperity as a trading and manufacturing nation.

Let us now turn to our criminal statistics.

3.—Crime.

United Kingdom.

Year.	Population.	Convictions.
1840 ...	26,487,026 ...	34,030
1850 ...	27,523,694 ...	41,008
1860 ...	28,778,411 ...	17,461
1870 ...	31,205,444 ...	18,401
1879 ...	34,155,126 ..	16,823
1880 ...	34,468,552 ..	15,643

Do these figures require a word of comment?
Let us now turn to the matter of education.

4.—Education.

United Kingdom.

Year.	Schools Inspected.	Accommodation	Average Attendance.
1863 ...	7,739 ...	1,512,782 ...	1,008,925
1869 ...	10,337 ...	2,076,344 ...	1,332,786
1874 ...	15,671 ...	3,344,071 ...	1,985,394
1879 ...	20,169 ...	4,727,853 ...	2,980,104
1880 ...	20,670 ...	4,842,807 ...	3,155,534

We thus see that while the material condition of our population has steadily improved, their moral and intellectual condition has also advanced in a remarkable degree.

One of the signs of improvement is in the matter of thrift. Take the Savings' Bank figures :—

5.—THRIFT.

In 1841 the deposits were...	...	...	£24,474,689
,, 1851 ,, ,,	...	...	...	30,277,654
,, 1861 ,, ,,	...	...	...	41,546,475
,, 1871 ,, ,,	...	...	...	55,844,667
,, 1879 ,, ,,	...	...	...	75,809,994
,, 1880 ,, ,,	...	...	...	77,721,084

6.—BANKRUPTCY.

In 1879 the insolvencies were in number 13,132, and in amount £29,678,000.

In 1880 the insolvencies were in number 10,298, and in amount £16,188,000.

7. TAXATION.

YEAR.	POPULATION.	AMOUNT RAISED.	PER HEAD.
1865 ...	29,861,908	... £70,313,436	... £2 7 1
1870 ...	31,205,444	... 75,434,252	... 2 8 4
1875 ...	32,749,167	... 74,921,873	... 2 5 9
1878 ...	33,799,386	... 79,763,298	... 2 7 2
1880 ...	34,468,552	... 81,265,055	... 2 7 1
1881 ...	34,788,814	... 84,041,288	... 2 8 4

INCOME TAX.

1869 Gross value of property and profits assessed	£434,804,000
1874 ,, ,, ,,	543,026,000
1879 ,, ,, ,,	578,046,000

8.—NATIONAL DEBT.

In 1870 this was ...	...	...	... £797,943,660
,, 1874 ,, ...	...	...	... 776,107,783
,, 1880 ,, ...	...	...	... 774,044,235
,, 1881 ,, ...	...	...	... 768,703,692

Let us now take Banking and the Clearing House returns :—

9.—BANKING.

June, 1880, Deposits at principal London Banks and Discount Companies	... £105,000,000
June, 1881 ,, ,, ,,	118,500,000

In 1870–71 the total Clearing was £4,018,464,000
„ 1878–79 „ „ „ 4,885,091,000
„ 1879–80 „ „ „ 5,265,976,000
„ 1880–81 „ „ „ 5,909,989,000

Do any of these figures give one an idea of decay?
Let us now look at our Railway traffics :—

10.—RAILWAYS.

Year.	Miles open.	No. of Passengers.	Total Receipts.	Per Mile.
1870	15,537	330,004,398	£45,078,143	£2,794
1875	16,658	506,975,234	58,982,753	3,541
1879	17,696	562,732,890	59,395,282	3,356
1880	17,945	603,884,752	61,958,754	3,453

Here again we have to notice the effects of the depression, and the indication of a fresh start, which the figures of 1880 afford. There is one thing, however, to be noted. Considering that since 1875 some 1,300 miles of comparatively unproductive lines have been built, we cannot but see that an enormous advance in the general prosperity has taken place in this department also.

Let us now take a few figures from our agricultural statistics :—

11.—AGRICULTURE.

Year.	Acres under Corn Crops.	Average price of Wheat.	No. of Cattle.	No. of Sheep.
1870	11,755,053	46s. 10d.	9,235,052	32,786,783
1877	11,103,196	56s. 9d.	9,731,537	32,220,067
1878	11,030,175	46s. 5d.	9,761,288	32,571,018
1879	10,777,459	43s. 10d.	9,961,536	32,237,958
1880	10,672,086	44s. 4d.	9,871,153	30,239,620

Here is the one bad exhibit in the national balance-sheet. Bad as these figures are, however, they do not, at first sight, convey any idea of the disastrous years, 1877, 1878, and 1879.

To obtain anything like a correct notion of the circumstances, it must be borne in mind that an almost total failure of crops, especially in 1879, was accompanied by very low market prices. The result was disastrous to the agricultural interest, and to every other interest which depended on it.

Landlords had to forego their **rents.** Farmers lost a great portion of their capital. Manufacturers lost the home markets. All **this** constituted our agricultural, and helped to constitute our commercial, depression.

Our working classes, however, owing **to the** bountiful harvests of America, were fed more cheaply **than** ever. And this has been, commercially and economically speaking, the salvation of the country.

I speak, of course, of the nation as a whole. Certain interests have suffered, and are suffering. The agricultural interest, and the manufacturing and commercial interests which depend on it, have suffered, and are still suffering, from the combined influences of bad harvests **and** low prices. But, large **and** important as these interests **are,** they cannot be allowed to outweigh the interests **of the** whole community.

As we have seen from all these facts and figures, it is quite possible **that** important interests may suffer, and yet that the community **as** a whole **may** be prospering. No Free Trader denies, or wishes to deny, that certain interests have suffered.

What the Free Trader asserts **is** that the **nation** as a whole is prosperous and thriving, and that **the proofs** abound on every side. The Neo-Protectionists **deny this;** but, in seeking to prove their case, they do not appeal to facts as a whole, but pick and choose those which appear to bear out their contention.

The facts, however, which they bring forward **never** do more than show that some particular interest **or** class is suffering, and this no one is concerned to **deny;** their facts never prove that the nation, **as** a whole, is suffering. In truth, every fact proves that **the** nation, **as** a whole, **is** very prosperous.

As a matter **of** course, the **classes** which suffer call out for relief. Agriculturists agitate **for** " Protection." Manufacturers clamour for " Reciprocity." I will discuss these matters in the following chapter.

IV.
"RECIPROCITY OR RETALIATION."

THIS is now the battle-cry of our Neo-Protectionists. They maintain that if foreigners keep out our products by hostile tariffs, we should threaten to do the same with theirs.

One of two things must happen : they will either open their ports, and we shall then have Reciprocity, or we shall close ours, and we shall then have Retaliation.

I have already discussed what might be the outcome of Reciprocity, that is free trade, to ourselves as a nation.

As regards the world at large, all are agreed upon the benefits that would ensue from an adoption of Free Trade. But, we might be driven to Retaliation, and that involves many important considerations which our Neo-Protectionists steadily keep out of view.

Let us look at some of these.

Let us assume that all the difficulties which might arise from " the most favoured nation " clause in existing treaties are obviated, and Retaliation pure and simple set up.

We should find ourselves in a most absurd and anomalous position.

Pray observe that when I use the terms " we," " us," " our," I mean the nation, the community, and not any particular class composing it. The distinction is an important one, but our Neo-Protectionists steadily ignore it. In discussing these questions it is found convenient by them, according to the exigencies of their argument, to use ambiguously the terms " we," and " us," and " our." When they use these terms, what is in their minds is, *some class and its supposed particular interests ;* which they would have you identify with *the nation and its general interests*—two things which may be diametrically opposed.

For this purpose " we " and " our " are convenient ambiguities.

The absurd and anomalous position in which we—that is the nation—should find ourselves is this :—The facts and figures I have adduced prove to demonstration that under the existing system of what our Neo-Protectionists are pleased to call one-sided Free Trade, and by means of it we, as manufacturers, and traders, have attained a position in the world which is at once the admiration, the envy, and, commercially speaking, the terror of competing nations ; yet, because some of our interests suffer from time to time in the fierce competition which has been engendered; and without pausing for a moment to estimate what benefits this same competition may in other respects have conferred on these very interests, they call in question our Free Trade policy ; they deny or ignore the results which it has attained for us ; and the nation is counselled to reverse that policy.

Each suffering interest has its noisy organs, its irresponsible chatterers. The agriculturist organs suggest duties on grain, but never hint at duties on other products. The manufacturing organs clamour for protective duties on the foreign products which compete with their own, but scout the notion of taxes on the food of the people, or on the raw material they use. Each one wants his own industry protected, while anxious that freedom shall rule in every other department.

It never seems to strike them that if Protection be once started, it must be extended to all commodities, and embrace all interests. It never seems to strike them that to protect one interest to the exclusion of the rest, is to commit a gross injustice. It never seems to occur to them that the interests, or supposed interests, of a class may be incompatible with, or opposed to, the interests of the community ; and that when this is the case, it is just and politic that the latter should prevail. They never seem to truly estimate such an elementary proposition as this : that however large and numerous a class may be, it forms only a part, and is not the whole of a nation.

Tried by these tests, what becomes of the cries which occasionally arise from some interest which may from time to time suffer from the universal competition, while the general progress of the nation is one onward march in the path of wealth and prosperity ?

The largest, the most important interest among us is agriculture. If any interest could claim protection as a matter of justice or policy, it is this. But, it was seen that to protect agriculture would be injurious to the general interest, and on this ground the Corn Laws were abolished.

The reasons which hold against Protection to agriculture apply with tenfold force to other and minor interests. If these interests clash with those of the community they must give way. There is no other possible method of attaining to the greatest happiness of the greatest number. And on no other ground can a Free Trader argue the question as regards Retaliation, or whatever form Protection may take ; whatever net gain it might bring to a class, the loss to the community would be much larger.

It must be contrary to the general interest that the price of any commodity should be artificially raised. To raise prices is, on the one hand, injurious to producers by checking consumption, and thus diminishing the demand for the article produced, and for the labour which produces it ; while on the other hand, it is injurious to the consumer, in forcing him either to pay more for, or to consume less of, the article of which he stands in need.

To diminish production is to diminish our industry, our trade, and our commerce, and thus to impoverish ourselves and the rest of the world.

It is the interest of the community that the keenest competition should reign, so that energy, enterprise, and invention shall have full play, and shall work for the benefit of ourselves and the rest of mankind. Protection dulls and stifles these beneficent forces, and its inevitable tendency is to bring about the mimimum of production at the maximum of cost. And on this ground it stands utterly condemned.

V.

TWO NEO-PROTECTIONISTS.

1. A Quarterly Reviewer, July, **1881**.
2. Sir Edward Sullivan, Bart., *Nineteenth Century*, August, 1881.

UNDER the head of "Imports and Exports" I have given a few extracts from two of the latest Protectionist utterances. I here take the opportunity of making a few comments on some of the facts relied on, and the conclusions drawn, in these two diatribes against Free Trade.

Let the reader turn to p. 7, *supra;* let him note the figures there given in a little calculation of three lines, and let him attentively consider the deductions which the Quarterly Reviewer draws from them, and the idea which he would give us of Sir Robert Peel's possible " dreams." First, as to his figures. What can be the writer's qualifications for discoursing on British Trade ? He does not seem to know or comprehend the meaning of " re-exports of foreign and colonial produce." If he did, he would not have made the egregious blunder of leaving out this item, which amounts to 63 millions. He makes out that the excess of our imports last year was 187 millions, but as he has taken no account of commodities merely passing through our ports, he overstates this excess by 63 millions ! Next, as to what Sir Robert Peel would have thought of a state of affairs which does *not* exist. If Sir Robert had lived in our day, and were as ignorant as this writer is, he might express alarm as this writer does, at the magnitude of our import trade. But Sir Robert had some acquaintance with the subject, and would not have been oblivious, or regardless, as this writer is, of the fact that Great Britain does more than half the world's ocean carrying trade, and that she has interest to receive on her foreign investments besides other trifles of this sort ; and that before she need do any bargaining as to her exports or imports, she has to receive from creation, by way of interest on loans, &c., and for work and labour done, in money, or in kind, considerably over 100 millions of pounds sterling a year ! No wonder a writer in *The Times* money article cites this blunder as " a measure of the intelligence of the new reciprocitarians."

Now for an instance of "hopeless muddle." In p. 291 of his article, the Quarterly Reviewer makes a kind of effort to explain how poor indebted England discharges this (according to him and his school) annually increasing adverse balance of trade. He says:—" We have about 2,000 millions invested in American and other foreign bonds, and with this we are paying for a large part of the difference between our imports and our exports. We are constantly told that gold is disappearing, and we know that instead of being an importer of the precious metal we are now obliged to export it. The theorists who uphold the wonderful dogma just referred to are lost in wonder over the 'drain of gold,' and are always asking some one to tell them what becomes of it. It goes towards the payment of our debts—that is the heart of the mystery. But this explanation does not satisfy the economists, and we find them, in despite of all evidence and reason, clinging hard and fast to an exploded delusion of an effete school, concocted during a period essentially different in all respects from the present." These are strong words. Let us look at them a little closer. He says we are paying our debts by selling our American and other foreign bonds.' Indeed ! If so, when did the process commence? There is not a single year, for the last twenty years, in which our imports have not exceeded our exports by at least 50 millions, the amount of the excess in the aggregate being something like 1,500 millions. And yet, at the end of this period, which comprises more than half the Free Trade epoch, and during which the country is said to have been getting rapidly impoverished, he makes out that we have in our strong box 2,000 millions of the world's obligations ! What can be this writer's idea of " evidence and reason ?" Both flatly contradict him. How did we get these 2,000 millions of bonds? We must have got at least half of them during the last twenty years. But during this time we had imported on balance over 100 millions of bullion ! How can we be getting in goods, bonds, and bullion from the rest of the world, owing nobody anything, and at one and the same time be impoverishing ourselves? But, he makes some obscure reference to a " drain of gold." Coupling this with his idea of our paying away our American and other bonds, I think I can pluck out what he calls " the heart of the mystery." It is matter of common knowledge that from 1877 to 1879, three years, European harvests were deficient and American harvests plentiful. The harvest of Europe in 1879 was about the worst ever known. This state of things was good for the United States, and bad for Europe. The demand for corn was enormous ; and as the United States had it to sell, they were enabled to turn it into money, and with the proceeds to do two most im-

portant things.   **They** had outstanding a debt on which
they were paying 5 and 6 per cent., and they were suffering
under an inconvertible currency.   During the nine years
1871—9 they had exported on balance £76,084,000
in gold.   Trade and commerce from 1873 to 1877 were
extremely depressed, more depressed than with us ;
but in a moment all was changed.   By means of the
vast supplies of grain they exported and sold to Europe,
they were enabled to pay off a considerable portion of
their debt, to reduce the interest on the remainder, and
to establish their currency on a metallic basis.   The
process adopted was to call in their bonds ; and to buy gold
in the markets of the world, as Italy, for a similar object,
is now doing.   Some of these bonds were held by us, some
by other nations ; we paid for them when we bought them
years before, and we got money or money's worth when we
parted with them.   As to the gold, some gold went away—
not more than we could easily spare, seeing that with an
increased volume of business money remains at from 2 to
2½ per cent.   In 1880-1 the United States imported on
balance £18,500,000 in gold ; but while Free Trading
England exported it to the extent of two to three millions
Protectionist France exported six or seven millions.   I
attach no importance to this fact, however, I only use it as
an *argumentum ad hominem ;* for gold, like everything else,
is a commodity, and tends to go where it is most wanted, and
can be paid for.   All that happened amounted to this, that
America, by the extraordinary coincidence of her possessing
three abundant harvests, while Europe suffered under three
deficient ones, was enabled to pay off some of her debt,
to reduce the interest on the remainder, and to put her
currency on a metallic basis.   All this should have been
within the ken of a writer who lays claim to "a mind
capable of comprehending facts," and who sets himself up
as an instructor on the Free Trade question.   But, all is
ignored, and we are made to carry away a dim sort
of idea that, in order to pay our way under our Free
Trade system, we are selling our bonds, and are being
drained of our gold ; a state of things which only exists in
the minds of such writers as this Quarterly Reviewer.

And now for another passage of his, p. 289 :—" Again,
if we look at the United States where Mr. Bright has so
often told us to look, we shall find that their exports for
the year ending June, 1881, exceeded their imports by
£54,000,000. This ought to mean that the Americans are
getting poorer, if they are not actually approaching bankruptcy ; but they by no means regard it in that light. They
like Mr. Bright's praises of their country, at the expense
of his own, but they will not have his teaching at any
price, and consequently they will go on exporting more
than they import as long as good fortune enables them to
do so. Then there is France, she also should have been
sinking deeper and deeper in the slough of despond, for
in her case also the exports exceed the imports."

This statement about France is astounding ! It is absolutely contrary to fact. In 1880 France, according to the
returns, imported in excess 63 millions ; in 1879, 57 millions ; and in 1878, 43 millions. France is now, and has
been for the last five years, an importer on balance, and
her annual excess imports are rapidly mounting.

Very severe things might be said of such a blunder as
this, but I pass on to his notions about the United States
excess of exports, which, by the way, was not 54 millions
but 52 millions, for the year ending in June last. His
notion that the wealth of the United States, and the virtues
of protection, are proved by this excess of exports is one
worthy of the Neo-Protectionist school, and "a measure of
their intelligence." Is our Quarterly Reviewer ignorant, or
is he oblivious, of the fact that the United States are largely
indebted to Europe, and have to pay a large annual tribute
to Europe, in money, or in kind, by way of interest on
that debt ; and that they have scarcely any ocean-carrying
trade ? Is he ignorant, or oblivious, of the fact that thousands
of absentees, and travellers, who come over here from the
States, have to remit to Europe, in one shape or other, the
expenses which they incur? Let us endeavour roughly to
estimate what these three items amount to.   1. Indebted-
ness.—Let us say the States owe Europe 500 millions ;
5 per cent on this makes 25 millions a year for them to pay
annually. 2. Shipping.—Owing to blessed Protection—poor

one-sided Free Trading England does most **of this** business
for them. They had not a single ocean grain-ship floating
last year, and they carried only 17½ per cent. **of** their
foreign commerce. Their export and import trade
amounted to 309 millions. Let us suppose for a
moment that on 82½ per cent. of this they paid 5 per
cent. for freight; this would make 12¾ millions more
to pay. Then there is the **item** of passenger fares
across the Atlantic, to and **fro.** Let us say half **a
million** for this. **3.** What shall **we** put down **for** the
10,000 absentees, **and** travellers, who flock to Europe
every year, and some **of** whom **are** among the richest men
in the world? Shall **we** say an average of £300? This
would give us **3** millions more. **There** may be other **items**
for works of art, jewellery, &c., but of them **I will** take **no**
account, so we will now sum up.

United States Annual Foreign Indebtedness, interest payable abroad...	£25,000,000
Ocean shipping charges ...	12,750,000
Absentees and travellers ...	3,000,000
	40,750,000

So that before the States can commence to talk about
exchanging a dollar's worth of their own products for a
dollar's worth of foreign products, they have to **pay** over
to Europe, in money or in kind, no less a sum than
40 millions sterling !

No wonder their exports exceed their imports ! What
ignorance, what folly, does it not betray, therefore, to build
up an argument in favour of Protection, and against Free
Trade, on the bare figures which appear in trade returns !
In the next chapter the reader will find the true deductions
which may be drawn from them.

Now **for Sir** Edward Sullivan in the *Nineteenth
Century.* **On** page 8, *supra,* will **be** found **two** passages
from his article, "Isolated **Free** Trade," to which I
would again **refer the** reader. They, and some further
extracts which I shall make, betray the fatuous ignorance concerning "imports and exports," which is the
characteristic of the whole school of Neo-Protectionists.

They all have the same notions about "foreigners flooding our markets with cheap and often nasty manufactured goods;" the same idea of "Free Trade increasing the balance of trade against us till it has reached the alarming figure of £136,000,000;" the same notion that we are "drawing upon our capital and our accumulated wealth."

But, there are other choice morsels which I must transcribe verbatim :—"The cloud that threatens the industrial existence of England has been gathering and intensifying for six years. 'Who,' asks Mr. Bright triumphantly, 'dare now propose a return to Protection?' 'Who,' it may be asked in return, 'amongst all the wise and acute and thoughtful men in enlightened Europe and America, dare now propose the adoption of Free Trade?' Not one; absolutely not one. After carefully watching the working of 'isolated' free trade in England for thirty years, they have unanimously, without a dissentient voice, rejected it as belonging to the puerile doctrines and illusions of mankind." "Practical thoughtful men are beginning to compare the prophecies and theories of free trade with the practical results, and they are aghast." "England is the only country in the world that has adopted what is called free trade, and England is the only country in the world that is retrograding in industrial prosperity." "Under protection America is accumulating annually £165,000,000. Under protection France is accumulating annually £75,000,000. Under Free Trade England is accumulating annually £65,000,000. Many experts maintain that since 1875—1876 she was losing money instead of accumulating. Protective America now exports more than she imports. Protective France imports annually £4,000,000 more than she exports. (The balance against her is £40,000,000 in ten years). Free trade England imports annually £130,000,000 more than she exports!"

Very few remarks are necessary on this farrago of reckless assertion and false inference.

It is not true that any cloud threatens the industrial existence of England, or that she is retrograding in industrial prosperity; facts abounding on every side point to the very opposite conclusion.

It is not true that wise, acute, and thoughtful men in Europe and America have unanimously, without a dissentient voice rejected Free Trade. I deny that any single "wise" man has done so, whatever any acute or thoughtful men—they are not necessarily wise—may have done. I deny that any but the merest sciolists are aghast at the practical results of Free Trade, for the simple reason that there is nothing in these results at which to be aghast. While, as to the prophecies which have been made as to the general acceptance of Free Trade by the nations within a certain limited time, it, may be conceded that the generous forecasts of its advocates have hitherto been unfulfilled. This, however, does not arise from the falsity of their doctrines, as the Protectionists would have it, but because of the prejudices and ignorance of men—such prejudices and ignorance for instance as these writers display—because of the existence of the self-same spirit which placed Galileo in prison for maintaining that the earth went round the sun ; and which consigned Giordano Bruno to the flames for asserting that the world was round.

And now I have to ask Sir Edward Sullivan for his authority for the figures given by him as to the respective annual "accumulations" of America, France, and England, in which England with £65,000,000 is placed at the bottom of the list with the remark that "many experts maintain that since 1875-1876 she was losing money instead of accumulating." I ask: who is his authority for such a statement?

Mr. Giffen, in one of his "Essays on Finance," 1878, puts down our "accumulations" for 1865—75 as £2,400,000,000, or £240,000,000 annually, and there is no reason for supposing that they have decreased since ; the figures given under "One-Sided Free Trade" proving the contrary. If there be any "expert" to set against the chief of the Statistical Department of the Board of Trade, I should like to know who he is, and on what factors he bases his calculation.

Then I have to ask him who is his authority for the statement that "Protective France imports annually, £4,000,000 more than she exports ;" and that "the balance against her is £40,000,000 in ten years ?"

On taking up Martin's "Statesman's **Year Book for** 1881,"
I find that, for the ten years ending 1879—the last year
given—the figures stand thus for her Imports and Exports :—

Imports for **Home** Consumption   ...   £1,494,713,400
Exports of Home **Produce**   1,387,392,480

Excess of Imports   107,320,920

But, **there** is last year, 1880, and I find that Mulhall in his
"Balance Sheet of the World" puts down France's excess
of imports for that year as **63** millions, which brings up
the total excess for eleven years to **170** millions !   In
1870, however, France exported on balance **3** millions, so
that the fact is that France **for** the last ten years has imported on balance, **on** the average, **17** millions, not **4** millions !
But, to stop **here** would be to give a very inadequate notion
of what France **is** doing in **the** way of imports and exports,
for I find that

In 1876 her excess imports were   ...   ... £**16**,500,000
    „ 1877   „   „   ...   10,800,000
    „ 1878   „   „   ...   43,600,000
    „ 1879   „   „   ...   57.200,000
    „ 1880   „   „   ...   63,000,000

So that France, though Protectionist, is actually, according
to our new school of writers, going **down** hill along with
free trading England !

But does it not seem extraordinary **that in** the face of
these figures we should be given to understand that France
imports annually only £4,000,000 more than she exports ?

At all events, he admits that France imports more than
she exports. But, **this** is in direct contradiction to his fellow
in the *Quarterly*, who, as we have seen, asserts that France
exports more than **she** imports ! These two Neo-Protectionists, therefore, are at direct variance with each other on
a matter of fact forming the very basis of their argument !

" *Arcades ambo*
Et cantare pares et respondere parati."

The only thing on which they are agreed is praise of
Protection and vilification of Free Trade.

Here I leave them, commending to them Mr. Glad-
stone's recent advice to Lord Randolph Churchill, to "avoid
facts **and logic,** and stick to rhetoric and declamation."

VI.

CONCLUSION.

And now let us endeavour to draw a few practical deductions from the foregoing discussion :—

1. That the fact of a nation's imports exceeding in value the exports, indicates, other things being equal, that this nation is a creditor of some other country.

2. And, conversely, that an excess of exports, other things being equal, indicates that the nation is an indebted nation.

3. That, among the older States, those who are advancing in wealth are gradually increasing their excess of imports, while in those which are economically decaying, there exists either an excess of exports, or a gradual decrease in excess of imports ; and that in proof of this we have only to examine the following figures, and to apply them to what is within common knowledge concerning the countries named :—

Great Britain, excess of imports,	1870,	59,000,000 ;	1880,	125,000,000.
France	,,	,,	1869,	3,000,000 ;	,, 63,000,000.
Holland	,,	,,	1870,	7,000,000 ;	,, 20,000,000.
Belgium	,,	,,	1870,	10,000,000 ;	,, 13,000,000.
Germany	,,	,,	1869,	12,000,000 ;	,, 6,000,000.
Russia	,,	exports,	1870,	4,000,000 ;	1878, 3,000,000.

4. That, among the younger nations, the United States stands out, at the present moment, as a great exporter on balance ; but that, as she is a heavily indebted nation, she cannot avoid exporting on balance until she has redeemed her obligations, and has recovered her share of the ocean-carrying trade , and that, consequently, to point, as Protectionists do, to her 52 millions of excess exports as, *ipso facto*, a proof of the virtues of their system, is to draw an unwarranted and mischievous conclusion.

5. That the term "Balance of Trade," as commonly used, is a misleading expression, calculated to give rise to the most absurd fallacies.

6. That the " Balance of Trade," if there be such a thing, is in favour of, and not adverse to, Great Britain.

7. That this " Balance " is likely to be more and more in our favour.

8. That the world is likely to become more and more indebted to us, and to pay us an annually increasing tribute in money, or money's worth.

9. That this state of things took its rise with the advent of Free Trade. and is distinctly traceable to it as a great efficient cause.

10. That the secret of our wealth lies in this, that our free imports give us an unmistakable advantage, as regards the element of cheapness, in the universal competition, and that the only way in which we can be deprived of this advantage is by other nations becoming Free Traders.

11. That it would be a very unwise thing, looking at it from a selfish point of view, to disturb this state of affairs by threatening other nations with hostile tariffs in retaliation for their prohibitory duties.

12. That if our threats were effective, other nations would immediately be put on the same basis as ourselves as regards cheapness of production, with a result, probably, anything but pleasant to us as traders, carriers, and manufacturers.

13. That if our threats were non-effective, we should, in this way, also put ourselves on a level with our competitors, with such accompaniments, however, as the following :—We should raise prices all round, and so diminish general consumption, and, consequently, production ; we should diminish our industry, our trade, and our commerce, and thus impoverish ourselves and the rest of the world, and, in doing so, we should imitate the very policy we condemn in foreigners.

14. That Free Trade is the best, nay, the only possible policy for us as a nation.

15. That some time or other, as sure as the day succeeds the night, the nations will discover that in establishing Free Trade, they secure the greatest happiness of the greatest number, and thus make a practical advance to a realisation of the benevolent motto of the Cobden Club—

"Peace and Goodwill among Nations."

August 15*th*, 1881.

www.ingramcontent.com/pod-product-compliance
Lightning Source LLC
Chambersburg PA
CBHW030915260626
47169CB00008B/2853